Meg Parker
and the
Mystery of the Old Book

Eleanor Robins

High Noon Books
Novato, California

Cover Design: Nancy Peach
Interior Illustrations: Herb Heidinger

Copyright ©1984, by High Noon Books, a division of Academic Therapy Publications, 20 Commercial Blvd., Novato, CA 94949-6191. All rights reserved. Printed in the United States of America. No part of this publication may be reproduced, stored in a retrieval system, or transmitted, in any form or by any means, electronic, mechanical photocopying, recording or otherwise, without the prior written permission of the publisher.

Glossary: hardly, excite

International Standard Book Number: 0-87879-444-1

8 7 6 5 4 3 2 1 0 9
5 4 3 2 1 0 9 8 7 6

Contents

CHAPTER 1

A Surprise for Kate

Meg was sitting on the front steps of her house. Kate, her best friend, walked over from her house across the street. They started to talk about Kate's birthday party.

"Who are you going to ask to your birthday party?" Meg asked.

"I want to ask Fred. But I don't think he will come," Kate answered.

"Why not?" Meg asked.

"I don't think he likes me," Kate said.

"Sure he does. He just isn't the kind of boy who tells who he likes," Meg said.

"I hope you're right. I sure do like him. Are you going to ask Dave?" Kate asked.

"I wouldn't ask anyone but him," Meg said.

"But you know he'll come because he likes you," Kate said.

"I have an idea. I'll ask Dave to drive Fred to your party. I'm sure Fred would come then," Meg said.

Kate said, "That's a great idea. Let's go to the Ice Cream Shop right now and ask them. You said they are both working there today."

"Do you want to see Fred? Or do you want some ice cream?" Meg asked.

Kate thought for a minute. Then she said, "Both."

"I'll write a note for Mom and Dad so they'll know where we are," Meg said.

"OK. I'll wait out here," Kate said.

Meg saw Mrs. Jones coming with the mail. She waited to get the mail before she went inside the house.

"Hi, Mrs. Jones," both Meg and Kate said.

"Hello, girls," Mrs. Jones said. She gave Meg some mail.

"Do you have any mail for me?" Kate asked.

Mrs. Jones said, "I sure do. This box is for you. Do you want it now? Or do you want me to take it and give it to your mom across the street?"

"I want it now. I can't wait to see what's in it," Kate said. She was very excited.

Mrs. Jones handed her the box.

Kate said, "Look, Meg. This is from my uncle Ed. It must be for my birthday. Uncle Ed has a store full of books. I bet this is a book. This box isn't very big. But it could hold a book."

"Let's go inside and open it," Meg said.

"OK. I can hardly wait. I wonder what kind of book it is," Kate said.

A man in a brown car was parked not far down the street from Kate's house. He was looking out his car window at the girls. But the girls didn't see him. They were too busy looking at the box.

CHAPTER 2

A Man Follows the Girls

The two girls hurried into the house. It took Kate a long time to get the box open. Then she pulled out what was inside the box. It really was a book.

"What kind of book is it?" Meg asked.

Kate didn't look very happy. "Why did Uncle Ed give me a book like this? Doesn't he know how old I am?"

Kate gave the book to Meg. Meg looked at it. Then she knew why Kate didn't like it. It was an old book about dolls.

Meg wanted Kate to feel better. She said, "It looks like a very nice book. I've never seen one just like this."

*Then she knew why Kate didn't like it.
It was an old book about dolls.*

Kate said, "But it's a book about dolls. I don't play with dolls anymore. Does Uncle Ed think I'm still a little girl? This is the kind of book your little sister Amy might like. And it's not even a new book."

"But it's still a nice book," Meg said. She gave the book back to Kate.

Kate put the book on the table. Then she said, "Hurry and write your note. I'm in a hurry to get to the Ice Cream Shop."

Meg wrote the note to her mom and dad. She wrote that she and Kate were going to the Ice Cream Shop.

Then Meg said, "OK, Kate. I'm ready to go. Come on."

"Is it OK for me to leave the old book on the table? I don't want to take it to the Ice Cream Shop," Kate said.

"Sure it is," Meg said. She got her keys. Then the girls started walking to the door. All of a sudden Meg stopped.

"What's wrong?" Kate asked.

"I just thought of something," Meg answered.

"What?" Kate asked.

"My uncle Bob wants to read one of Dad's books. We could stop at the Police Station on our way to the Ice Cream Shop. Then I could give it to him. Can I have your box to put it in?" Meg said.

Kate said, "Sure. But can we stop by there after we go to the Ice Cream Shop? I don't think I can wait much longer to ask Fred to my party."

Meg got the box and the book. She put the book inside the box.

The two girls hurried outside. Meg locked the front door. Then the two girls quickly walked to Meg's old green car and got in. Kate put the box on the front seat next to her and Meg. Then Meg backed out on to the street.

The girls were busy talking. They didn't see the man sitting in the brown car not far from Kate's house.

But the man saw Meg's car go down the street. Then he started to follow them.

CHAPTER 3

Fred Gives His Answer

Meg turned left on Main Street. Then she turned into the parking lot next to the Police Station. The girls got out of the car and locked it.

The man in the brown car parked his car not far from Meg's car.

The girls walked very quickly by the Police Station. Kate was carrying the box with the book in it. They hurried inside the Ice Cream Shop. Dave and Fred were both busy. There were a lot of people in the Shop.

Meg and Kate walked over to a table. Kate put the box on the table. She said, "You ask Dave first. Then I'll ask Fred. I'll go read the notes on the wall while you ask Dave."

A lot of people put notes on one of the walls at the Ice Cream Shop. Many of the notes were about jobs.

Dave came over to Meg. He said, "What kind of ice cream can I get you and Kate?"

"Surprise us," Meg said.

"I was hoping you would come in today," Dave said.

"Why?" Meg asked. But she thought she knew why.

"I just wanted to see you," Dave answered.

Meg thought that was what he would say. His answer made her very happy.

"What's in the box?" Dave asked.

"A book of Dad's that my uncle Bob wants to read," Meg answered.

"I better go get the ice cream," Dave said. He started to walk away.

Meg said, "Wait, Dave. I have something to ask you."

"What?" Dave asked.

"Kate's birthday is in a few days. Her mom and dad are having a birthday party for her. Can you come to the party?" Meg asked.

"Are you going to be there?" he asked.

"Sure I am," Meg said.

"Then you know I'll be there. I wouldn't miss it. Should I bring Kate something?" Dave asked.

Meg said, "No. But Kate sure would like for you to bring someone with you."

"Another girl?" Dave asked.

"Oh, Dave," Meg said.

They both laughed.

"Who?" Dave asked.

"Fred. Will you tell Fred you'll drive him to the party in your car?" Meg asked.

"Sure. Is Kate going to ask him to the party? Or do I have to?" Dave asked.

"She's going to ask him. We just want you to tell him you'll bring him," Meg said.

"I'll be glad to do it. I'll tell him to bring your ice cream over. Then Kate can ask him," Dave said.

Dave walked over to Fred. Kate walked back to the table and sat down with Meg.

"What did Dave say?" Kate asked.

"He said he'd bring Fred to your birthday party. And he's going to get Fred to bring our ice cream over. So you can ask Fred then," Meg said.

Dave talked to Fred for a few minutes. Then he gave him the two dishes of ice cream. And he gave Fred a little push.

Slowly Fred came over to the table. "Here's the ice cream," he said.

Meg looked at Kate. Kate didn't say anything. Meg looked at Kate again. Then she gave Kate a little kick under the table.

Meg looked at Kate again. Then she gave Kate a little kick under the table.

Kate said, "Fred, I have something to ask you."

"What?" Fred asked. But he looked like he already knew what it was.

"My birthday is in a few days. My mom and dad are having a party for me. Can you come?" Kate asked.

"Sure. See you then," Fred said. Then he walked back over to where Dave was.

Kate was excited. She said, "He's coming to my birthday party!"

"I told you he would," Meg said.

A man walked into the Ice Cream Shop. He was the man in the brown car. He sat down at the table next to Meg and Kate.

CHAPTER 4

Something Is Wrong

The girls started to eat the ice cream. Then Kate said, "What am I going to talk to Fred about at my party?"

Meg said, "You'll think of something. You could tell him about your uncle sending you the old book."

"I'm not going to tell him I got a book about dolls. He might laugh," Kate said.

"But you'd know he was having a good time," Meg said.

The man at the next table got up. He walked over to Meg and Kate. He looked at Kate. Then he said, "Did I hear you say you had a book about dolls?"

"Yes, you did," Kate said.

There was something about the man that Meg didn't like. But she didn't know what it was.

The man said, "I'd like to buy the book for my little girl. She likes dolls very much. Is the book in this box on the table?"

Kate said, "No, it isn't. I left it at my friend Meg's house. But I can't let you buy the book. My uncle Ed gave it to me."

"That's all right. I'll get one somewhere else," the man said.

All of a sudden the man seemed in a hurry to go. He hurried out of the Ice Cream Shop without buying any ice cream.

Meg was glad he left.

"What are you going to wear to your birthday party?" Meg asked.

"I'm not sure. Mom's going to buy me a new dress. What are you going to wear?" Kate said.

"I don't know. My mom might buy me a new dress, too," Meg answered.

"I have an idea. Let's go look at dresses at the shop next door. We might find some dresses there to wear to my birthday party. Then we can tell our moms about them," Kate said.

"OK," Meg said.

The girls hurried and ate the ice cream.

Dave and Fred didn't come back over to the table. They stayed busy working.

The girls put the money for the ice cream on the table. Kate picked up the box. Then they left the Ice Cream Shop.

They walked next door to the dress shop. They looked around for a long time. They saw a lot of dresses that they liked.

Meg said, "We need to go, Kate. My mom and dad may be home by now. We need to get back to my house before they start to worry about us. We can come back another afternoon with our moms."

"OK," Kate said.

The girls left the dress shop. They walked to the Police Station. They went inside to give the book to Meg's uncle Bob.

Meg said, "Oh, no. That's my house. Come on, Kate. I have to get home right away."

Meg walked over to a policeman. She said, "I want to see Chief Parker."

The policeman said, "Chief Parker isn't here right now. He had to hurry over to his brother's house. Something is wrong there."

Meg said, "Oh, no. That's my house. Come on, Kate. I have to get home right away."

CHAPTER 5

The Man Follows the Girls Again

The two girls ran to the parking lot. Meg unlocked her car, and they quickly got in. Meg was worried.

Kate said, "Don't worry, Meg. I'm sure everything is all right at your house. Maybe the policeman didn't hear what your uncle really said when he left."

"I hope you're right," Meg said.

Meg was in a hurry to get home. But she was careful not to drive too fast. It seemed to take a long time to get to her house.

Meg saw her uncle's police car parked in front of her house. Meg parked her car. Then they got out and rushed into the house. Kate had the box with the book in it.

Meg's mom and dad and her uncle Bob were in the kitchen. They were sitting at the table.

"Mom, Dad, are you all right?" Meg asked.

"Don't worry, Meg. We're all OK," her mom said.

Meg turned to her uncle Bob. She said, "We went by the Police Station to see you. One of the policemen said you'd hurried over here because something was wrong here. I've been very worried."

Her uncle said, "That is why I came over

here. But I'm sorry my policeman told you that. I know how worried you must have been."

Kate said, "Mr. and Mrs. Parker and Amy are all right. So what's wrong?"

Meg's dad said, "A man was trying to get in the house when we got home. He ran around in back of the house when he saw us. I ran after him, but he got away. I don't know where he went. I'm just glad you two girls weren't here."

"Why was he trying to get in the house?" Meg asked.

"We don't know," her dad answered.

"Did you two girls see a man anywhere around here before you left? Or a car that shouldn't have been here?" her uncle asked.

"No, we didn't," Kate said.

"But we were only looking for cars going down the street. We were too busy talking to see any others," Meg said.

"He may not have been here when you left. Don't worry about the man trying to get in the house again. I'll have my policemen out looking for him," Meg's uncle Bob said.

"Thanks, Bob," Meg's dad said.

Meg's uncle Bob said, "Meg, why did you and Kate go by the Police Station? Was it to talk to me about something? Or just to say hello?"

Meg said, "I almost forgot with everything going on. We went by to take you the book of Dad's that you wanted to read."

Kate gave the box with the book in it to Meg's uncle. She said, "We put it in the box my book came in."

Meg's mom looked down at the book on the table. She said, "Is that your old book about dolls, Kate? I wondered where it came from."

Meg said, "Kate's uncle sent it to her for her birthday."

"I don't know why my uncle sent it to me. He must have forgotten how old I am. I haven't played with dolls in a very long time," Kate said.

Meg's mom said, "Maybe he thought you'd like to read about the dolls."

Meg's uncle got up from the table. "I have to get back to the Police Station. I'll be back later."

"OK. I'll walk you to your car," Meg's dad said.

The two men walked outside.

Meg's mom said, "Meg, can you go to the grocery store for me? I need you to buy a few things."

"Sure, Mom. I'll be glad to," Meg said.

"I'll go with you," Kate said.

Meg's mom told Meg what she wanted at the grocery store. Then Meg and Kate started to the door.

Kate stopped. "Wait, Meg. I might as well take my old book with me."

The girls went outside to Meg's car. Kate was carrying the old book.

Meg's uncle Bob had already gone. Meg's dad was walking around in back of the house.

The girls got in Meg's car. Kate put the old book on the front seat next to her and Meg.

Meg didn't see any cars coming down the street. She didn't see the man in the brown car. He had just parked his car not far down the street from Kate's house.

Meg backed out. Then she started driving to the grocery store.

The man in the brown car started to follow the two girls.

CHAPTER 6

The Old Book Is Stolen

Meg and Kate didn't know that the man in the brown car was following them.

Kate said, "Why do you think that man wanted to get in your house?"

"I don't know. I'm just glad Dad got there before he got inside," Meg said.

"I'm glad he did, too," Kate said.

"I don't even want to think about it. Let's talk about something else. It gives me the creeps," Meg said.

"OK. What do you want to talk about?" Kate asked.

"Anything but about that man trying to get in my house," Meg answered.

"Then let's talk about my birthday party some more," Kate said.

"OK," Meg said.

"I can hardly wait for the party," Kate said.

"And I know why," Meg said.

"Why?" Kate asked.

"Because Fred said he would come," Meg said.

"I'm so glad he said he would," Kate said.

Meg laughed. "I know. You've told me that many times already."

"But I wasn't sure he'd say he would," Kate said.

"I was," Meg said.

Meg turned into the parking lot at the grocery store. The man in the brown car turned into the parking lot after them.

Meg parked her car. She said, "Are you going to take your book in, Kate?"

"No. I'm going to leave it in the car," Kate answered.

"Do what you want to do. But it isn't a good idea to leave it in the car. Someone might take it," Meg said.

"No one would want to take an old book about dolls," Kate said.

The girls got out of the car. Meg locked her door. But Kate forgot to lock her door. The girls started walking to the grocery store.

The man in the brown car went by the girls and looked at them. Then he went to park his car. He had to park a long way from Meg's car. He got out of his car and started walking to Meg's car.

The girls hurried inside the grocery store. They got the few things Meg's mom wanted. Then they hurried back to Meg's car.

A man was getting into Meg's car.

"Get out of my car," Meg yelled to the man.

The man got out of the car and started running away.

"Look at that," Meg yelled.

Kate said, "That's the man from the Ice Cream Shop. He has my old book!"

"Get out of my car," Meg yelled to the man.

CHAPTER 7

The Man Gets Away

Both girls started running after the man. The man was running very fast. He turned around to see where the girls were, and he ran into another man. He didn't fall. But he dropped the old book. It went under someone else's car.

The man kept running. The girls stopped to get the old book. They saw the man get in a brown car and drive out of the parking lot.

Kate got under the car and got her book. "Why would anyone want this old book?"

Meg said, "I don't know. But I'm going to try to find out. The first thing I'm going to do is call Uncle Bob from a pay phone. I bet that's the same man who tried to get in my house."

Meg hurried to a pay phone. She called the Police Station. Her uncle came to the phone right away. "What's wrong, Meg? Has that man been back to your house?"

Meg said, "No, Uncle Bob. Kate and I are at the grocery store. A man took Kate's old book out of my car. He dropped the book and we got it back. But we think he's the same man who tried to get in the house."

"Why do you think that?" her uncle asked.

Meg told him about seeing the man in the

Ice Cream Shop. She told him about the man trying to buy Kate's book. Then she said, "Kate told him she left the book at my house. Not long after that a man tried to get in my house. I think that man knew where Kate and I lived. I think he's been following us."

"Did you see where the man went? Do you have any ideas on where he might go?" her uncle asked.

Meg said, "We saw him drive out of the parking lot in a brown car. Then he made a right turn onto First Street."

"Go back to your house, Meg. I'll meet you there as soon as I can. And be careful," her uncle said.

Meg told him she would. She hung up the phone. Then she looked over at Kate. "Uncle Bob wants us to meet him at my house. He'll be there as soon as he can."

The two girls hurried to Meg's car. Meg was in a hurry. But she made herself drive very carefully.

Soon they were back at Meg's house.

Kate said, "This time I'm not going to leave my book in the car. I'm taking it inside with me."

CHAPTER 8

An Answer to the Mystery

The girls got out of the car and started walking to the house. Meg was carrying the things her mom wanted. Kate was carrying her old book. They walked inside the house and went to the kitchen.

Meg's mom said, "What took you so long? I was starting to worry about you."

Meg told her mom about the man in the brown car.

"I'm glad he didn't hurt you two girls. How did he get in your car?" Meg's mom said.

Kate said, "I forgot to lock the door on my side."

"I'm just glad you two girls are all right," Meg's mom said.

"Uncle Bob said he'd meet us here as soon as he could. I hope he can help us find out what is going on," Meg said.

It was a long time before Meg's uncle Bob came.

"What took you so long, Uncle Bob?" Meg asked when he came into the house.

"I've been busy finding out what's been going on. And busy finding the man in the brown car," he answered.

"Did you find the man?" Meg asked.

Meg's uncle said, "I sure did. And he told me everything. He was the man who tried to get in this house. He was trying to get the old book."

"He was the man who tried to get in this house. He was trying to get the old book."

"How did you find him so quickly?" Kate asked.

Meg's uncle said, "Your uncle Ed helped me. I saw his name and the name of his store on the box you gave me. I called him at his store. I told him what had been going on here. He knew that one of the men who works for him drives a brown car. He told me the man's name. I got the man's car tag number. Then we found him very quickly."

"Why did the man want the book?" Meg asked.

Meg's uncle said, "The book is worth a lot of money. Kate's uncle told the man to put a book about old dresses in the box. He thought Kate might like to see what women used to wear. But the man put the old book about dolls in the box. The man was planning to get the book away from Kate without anyone knowing who took it. But you girls didn't let him get the book."

"I'm sure glad we didn't," Kate said.

"Kate, your uncle will be here in a few days to get the book about dolls. And to bring your book about old dresses," Meg's uncle said.

"Thanks for the help," Meg said.

"Any time, Meg. I'm just glad we got an answer to this mystery," her uncle said.

Meg's uncle left, and the two girls sat down on Meg's front steps. They talked about the man in the brown car and the old book about dolls.

Then Kate said, "I've been thinking some more about what to wear to my birthday party. Maybe I shouldn't buy a new dress to wear. Maybe I should buy some nice new jeans. What do you think, Meg?"

"I don't know. Maybe that is a good idea. But we still have some time to think about it. But I am sure of one thing," Meg said.

"What?" Kate asked.

"Your party may be exciting. But it isn't going to be as exciting as this afternoon was," Meg answered.

"Maybe not. But it sure is going to be a lot more fun," Kate said.